THE SMURFS 2

adapted by Farrah McDoogle
illustrated by Dynamo Limited

The Smurfs in Paris

SIMON SPOTLIGHT
An imprint of Simon & Schuster Children's Publishing Division
1230 Avenue of the Americas, New York, New York 10020
For information about special discounts for bulk purchases,
please contact Simon & Schuster Special Sales at 1-866-506-1949 or business@simonandschuster.com.
Manufactured in the United States of America 0513 LAK
First Edition
2 4 6 8 10 9 7 5 3 1
ISBN 978-1-4424-8993-6

It was a beautiful day in Smurf village. The Smurfs were feeling especially smurfy because it was Smurfette's birthday, but they were planning a surprise party for her, so they pretended to have forgotten all about it. They were such smurfy actors that Smurfette believed them.

Maybe I really don't belong here. No one remembered my Smurfday, thought Smurfette sadly as she headed for a walk in the woods all by herself.

Meanwhile, in Paris, France, the evil wizard Gargamel was plotting to capture Smurfette. Once he had her, he planned to force her to give him Papa Smurf's secret formula for creating Smurfs. With the formula, Gargamel could create all the Smurfs he wanted to, and steal their precious, magical Smurf essence.

Gargamel used some of his small supply of essence to create a portal at the top of the Eiffel Tower. But the portal was too small for him to fit through. Gargamel had created Vexy and her brother, Hackus, to be very naughty . . . so naughty, in fact, that he called them the Naughties. Gargamel sent Vexy through the portal to capture Smurfette and bring her back to Paris.

Vexy was only too happy to follow her father, Gargamel's, orders. The portal took her to Smurf Village, where she found Smurfette! She grabbed Smurfette's arm and smurfnapped her, pushing her through the portal and back to Paris . . . where Gargamel was waiting.

The other Smurfs heard Smurfette scream and arrived in time to see her go through the portal. But they didn't know where she was being taken.

Papa Smurf knew just what to do. "We will use magic smurfportation crystals to go to Master Winslow's apartment mushroom. If anyone can help us find Smurfette, it will be Master Winslow and Grace!"

When Smurfette arrived in Gargamel's hotel suite in Paris, she was feeling very scared, but she acted brave. "You're wasting your time!" she told Gargamel. "Papa and the others will come rescue me!"

"I don't think so," Gargamel snarled. "After all, you're not a real Smurf! You're *my* creation, remember?"

Gargamel hit on Smurfette's deepest, darkest fear. What if Gargamel was right and she wasn't a true-blue Smurf? And what if the Smurfs tried but couldn't find her?

Things weren't looking very smurfy for Smurfette in Paris . . . but lucky for her, Papa Smurf was right about Patrick and Grace being able to help.

"It won't be hard to find Gargamel," Patrick explained to the Smurfs. "He's a big star now. In Paris!"

And so, Papa Smurf, Brainy, Vanity, Clumsy, Grouchy, Patrick, Grace, Blue, and Patrick's stepfather, Victor, all rushed to the airport to catch the next plane. Soon they arrived in Paris!

Paris is a very big city, so it was a good thing that Gargamel was so famous. A newspaper showed a picture of him in front of the hotel he was staying in. It was also easy to find out where Gargamel performed his magic shows because they were so popular. The Smurfs knew they would find Gargamel in one of those two places in Paris: his hotel or the opera house.

"Are we clear on the plan?" asked Patrick.

It was time to rescue Smurfette!

The Smurfs headed to the opera house first. Gargamel was performing onstage and had left Smurfette tied up in his dressing room. She was being guarded by Vexy and

Meanwhile, the Smurfs snuck past the guards and crept toward Gargamel's dressing room. They almost got there in time to rescue Smurfette . . . but at the same exact time, she was figuring out a way to escape.

"Oh no! Get her!" cried Vexy as she saw Smurfette getting away.

Smurfette ran through the streets of Paris trying to get away from the Naughties. It was such a busy city, so different from Smurf Village, that Smurfette wasn't sure where to go. Meanwhile, Vexy and Hackus were right behind her.

Vexy convinced Hackus to go inside the candy store and get into trouble. "We have to help him!" Vexy cried, tricking Smurfette into saving him. Smurfette hesitated, but only for a moment. Hackus and Vexy might be working for Gargamel, but they needed her help! So Smurfette did the smurfy thing and helped Hackus escape. She was surprised at how much fun she was having with the Naughties, and wondered if maybe she was a bit naughty after all.

The Naughties and Smurfette returned to the hotel. When Gargamel saw Smurfette getting along so nicely with the Naughties, he believed that his evil plan was working. Soon he would have the formula from Smurfette and all the essence he needed to become the most powerful wizard in the world!

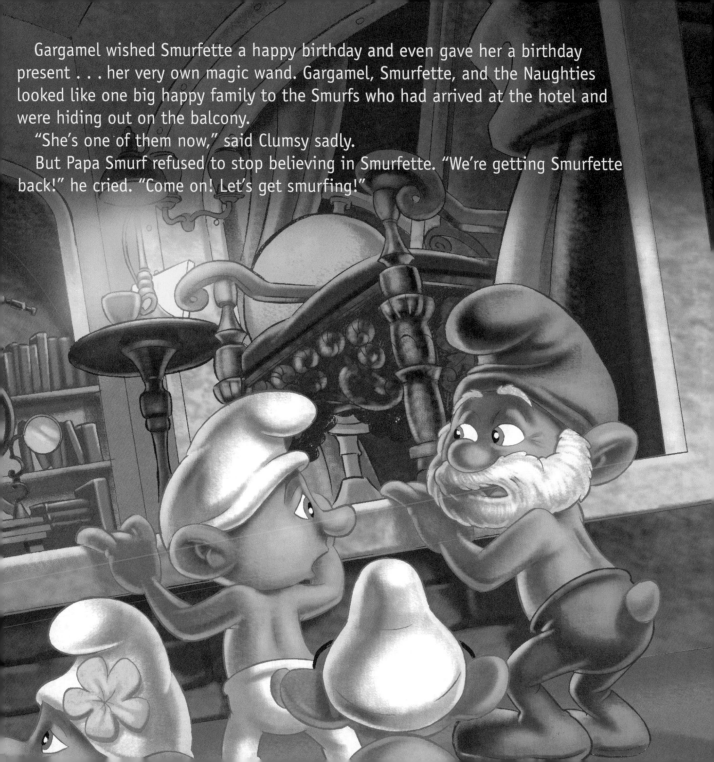

Gargamel wished Smurfette a happy birthday and even gave her a birthday present . . . her very own magic wand. Gargamel, Smurfette, and the Naughties looked like one big happy family to the Smurfs who had arrived at the hotel and were hiding out on the balcony.

"She's one of them now," said Clumsy sadly.

But Papa Smurf refused to stop believing in Smurfette. "We're getting Smurfette back!" he cried. "Come on! Let's get smurfing!"

Gargamel told Smurfette and the Naughties that he was taking them out to celebrate Smurfette's birthday, but instead took them to his underground lair. As soon as she saw the giant Smurfalator, Smurfette knew that Gargamel had lied and that they were in trouble. Gargamel threatened to hurt the Naughties if Smurfette didn't tell him Papa's formula.

But the other Smurfs hadn't given up searching for Smurfette! They found a Smurf-size storm drain that took them far below the streets of Paris to Gargamel's secret laboratory.

Patrick and Victor couldn't fit, so they found a human-size manhole and climbed in. "We'll see you down there!" called Patrick as the Smurfs disappeared into the drain.

When the Smurfs found the secret lair, they watched from above as Smurfette told Gargamel the recipe for Papa's formula. She couldn't let her new brother and sister die!

But Gargamel's victory didn't last long. Just in the nick of time, Patrick, Victor, and the Smurfs found a way to smurf with Gargamel's Smurfalator so it wouldn't work!

"Son of a smurf!" cried Gargamel as he stomped out the door to try and find out what had gone wrong.

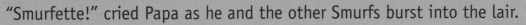

"Smurfette!" cried Papa as he and the other Smurfs burst into the lair.
"You came for me?" asked Smurfette in disbelief.
"Of course we came for you!" replied Papa Smurf. "Was there ever any question?"

Papa and Vanity worked together to free Smurfette from the Smurfalator.

"What about them?" Smurfette asked, pointing to the Naughties.

"They're Gargamel's!" replied Grouchy.

"But you never gave up on me . . . and I'm not giving up on them!" cried Smurfette.

"And you thought you weren't a Smurf!" exclaimed Papa Smurf.

And so, the Smurfs and the Naughties escaped from Gargamel's clutches . . . with a little help from their human friends! Then Smurfette used her magic wand to smurf enough crystals for all the Smurfs to return home to Smurf Village . . . but not before saying a big thank you to Patrick and his family for coming to her rescue in Paris!